Olga Visits Her Grandparents

Featuring Olga the Chicken

Created, Written, and Photographed by
C. L. Maxfield

This book is dedicated to
My parents and grandparents.

Olga the Chicken jumped out of bed.
She quickly ate breakfast,
Then put a hat on her head.

Today she was going
To her Grandparent's house.
She was excited to see them-
She was leaving the hen house!

Olga walked in the woods
Through the fallen leaves.
It was quiet and peaceful,
Not another critter to be seen.

Olga arrived at the farm down the road.
She spotted her Grandpa,
Talking with a toad!

When Grandpa saw Olga
He gave her a hug.
Then he reached in his pocket
And pulled out a candy bug!

Olga looked around the corner
And Grandma was there.
She was a fine hen.
She had style and flair.

Olga played with her Grandparents
For the rest of the day.
She was so tired by nightfall
She decided to stay.

She woke up in the morning
To wonderful smells.
Grandma had made her favorite breakfast –
Snails fresh from the shells!

After breakfast they washed
All the dishes and cups.
Then Olga helped sweep
And spruce the place up!

Olga had a nice visit.
She loved them so much!
She promised to call them,
And always keep in touch.

Olga enjoyed
The short walk home.
The woods were quiet,
But she never felt alone.

Her friends had missed her.
They welcomed her back.
She told them her stories,
And they all shared a snack.

Olga was happy.

I hope you enjoyed this book.

Find Olga the Chicken on Facebook!

Bye for now!

Made in the USA
Middletown, DE
12 November 2021